What's In A Doctor's Bag?

Written by Neil Shulman and Sibley Fleming

Illustrated by Todd Stolp

To those who conceived or were conceived
by the authors —
Clyde and Dotte Stolp
Vincent and Wolfie Fleming
Sonnie and Mary Shulman

Books by Neil Shulman and Todd Stolp, illustrated by Todd Stolp
What's in a Doctor's Bag?
The Germ Patrol: All About Shots for Tots... and Big Kids, Too!

Other Books by Neil Shulman
The Backyard Tribe
Better Health Care for Less
The Black Man's Guide to Good Health
Doc Hollywood (originally What? Dead... Again?)
Finally... I'm a Doctor
High Blood Pressure
Let's Play Doctor
Life Before Sex
101 Ways To Know If You're a Nurse
Second Wind
Under the Backyard Sky
Understanding Growth Hormone
What? Dead... Again? (The original version of Doc Hollywood)

Copyright © 1994 Neil Shulman and Todd Stolp
Illustrations © Todd Stolp and Neil Shulman
Second paperback edition, 1998, RxHumor
All rights reserved.

Library of Congress Cataloging-in-Publication Data
Shulman, Neil.
What's in a doctor's bag? / written by Neil Shulman and Sibley
Fleming; illustrated by Todd Stolp.
p.   cm.
ISBN 0-9639002-3-4
1. Children—Medical examinations—Juvenile literature.
2. Children—Preparation for medical care—Juvenile literature.
[1. Medical care.   2. Medical instruments and apparatus.]
I. Fleming, Sibley.   II. Stolp, Todd, ill.   III. Title
RJ50.5.S57 1994
610--dc20   94-25378

Published in the United States of America.

To order books, write or call:
Rx Humor
2272 Vistamont Drive
Decatur, GA 30033
Tel: (404) 321-0126/Fax: (404) 633-9198
Email: nshulma@emory.edu
www.dochollywood.com

Printed in Hong Kong.

What's in a Doctor's Bag ?

Written by
Neil Shulman
and
Sibley Fleming
Illustrated by
Todd Stolp

℞ Humor
Atlanta

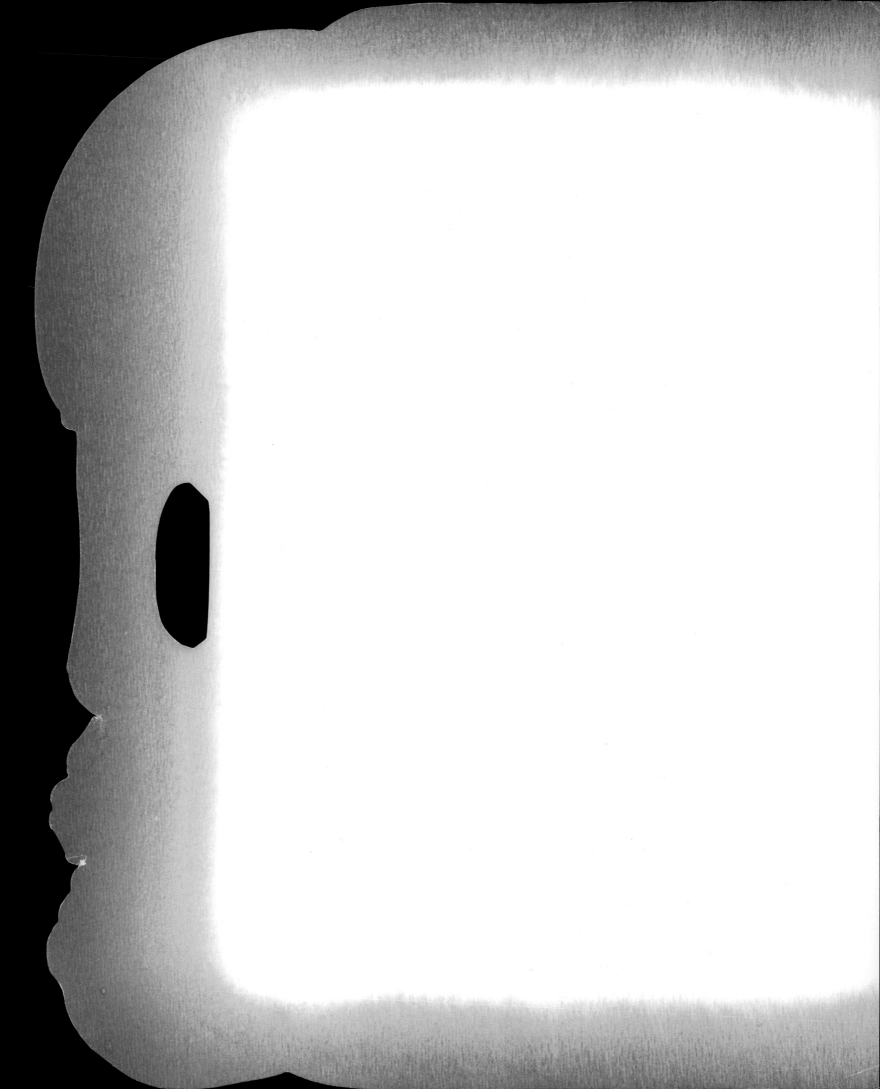

Once upon a time there was a big, tall doctor ...

...and a small little boy who had an earache in his ear.

6

One day, the boy's mother took him to the doctor's office for a check-up. The boy was very scared that the check-up would hurt more than the earache.

When the boy's mother left the room to fill out
some forms, the doctor scooted forward. "Let's just
have a look at that ear," said the doctor.

He pulled out an instrument from his black bag, but the instrument's top wouldn't shut. The batteries kept plopping out every time he tried to close the lid.

The doctor got so flustered when the batteries wouldn't stay put...

10

...he gave up and went to get an instrument that worked.

The boy was left all alone. He jumped off the table and accidently tipped over the doctor's black bag. All the instruments inside spilled onto the floor.

Suddenly, the boy heard a tiny voice. He thought it said, *"Ouch!"*

The little boy's eyes opened wide! He closed them and rubbed them, but what he saw was still there.

The instruments stood up, brushed themselves off, and pulled themselves together! After being cramped up in that old black bag for so long they were very glad to be able to stretch.

13

"Allow me to introduce myself," said one instrument who looked like he came from a spaceship. "I'm Otis. I'm an **o-to-scope** or an **oph-thal-mo-scope**. Depends on what you want to see."

"You must have hit your head!" said the boy. "You can't be *two* things at the same time! You have to be *one* or the *other*."

14

"Let me explain," offered Otis. "When I cock my head this way, I am an **o-to-scope**. I help the doctor to look into your ears so he can see if there are any germs making the ear drums red and sore."

"Doesn't that *hurt*?" asked the boy.

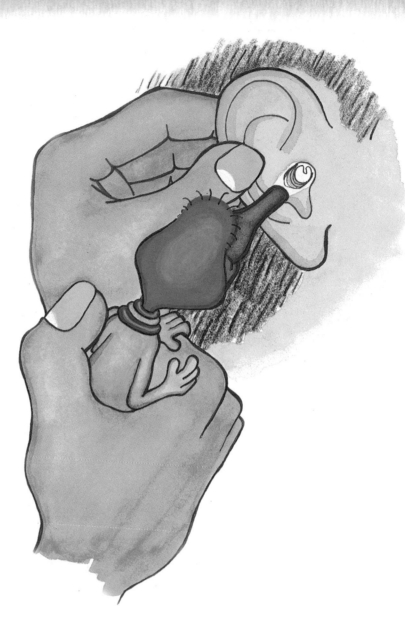

All the instruments laughed.

"No, of course not," answered Otis. "I'm just looking in your ear."

"And when are you the *other* thing?" asked the boy.

The instrument cocked his head back the other way. *"Hokus pokus!* I'm one now."

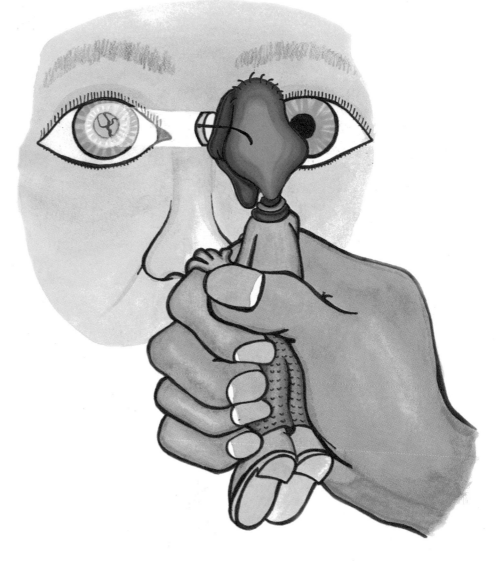

"I can see all kinds of things way in the back of your eyes like tubes that carry blood to feed your eyes and the nerves that help you see."

"Whoa! Wait a minute! Doesn't *that* hurt?" asked the boy.

The instruments roared with laughter.

18

"Why of all the silly things," said another
instrument wiggling forward. "I bet you're scared of
steth-o-scopes too." The **steth-o-scope** was very
proud of his work.

"I'm Lubba. He's Dubba. We're the only ones in
the doctor's bag who can hear."

19

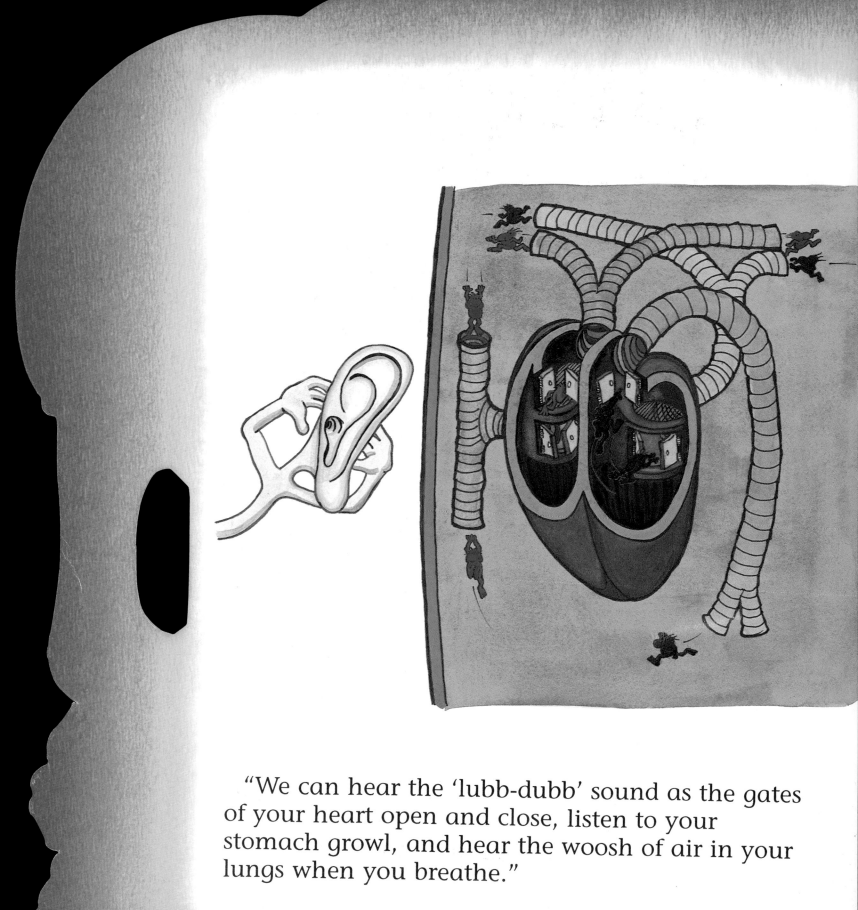

"We can hear the 'lubb-dubb' sound as the gates of your heart open and close, listen to your stomach growl, and hear the woosh of air in your lungs when you breathe."

20

All the instruments made a loud 'wooshing' sound and became so wild that the reflex hammer had to tap on the floor to bring them back to order.

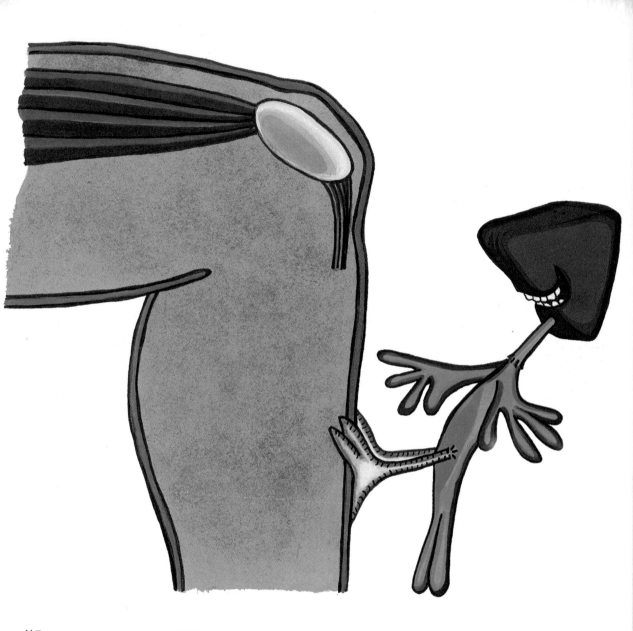

"Just a second!" said the boy when he saw the reflex hammer. "What do *you* do? You look scary."

The reflex hammer cleared her voice in order to sound important. "No way! I'm the most fun of them all," she said.

"You can call me Ms. Kneeknocker. I help the doctor to lightly tap on different joints so that he can see your legs jump up. This tells him that your body's electrical system is in tip top shape."

Suddenly the boy felt something squeeze his arm.

"Bet you can't guess what *my* job is?" said the instrument wrapped around his arm.

"They call me B.P. for short. Mr. B.P. Cuff, that is." The boy was surprised that the instrument didn't seem to hurt at all.

24

"I squeeze your arm like this, and from this round gauge, the doctor can tell how much power it takes for your heart to pump blood through your body."

"My job is really fun because I get to hug your arm — it's so silly."

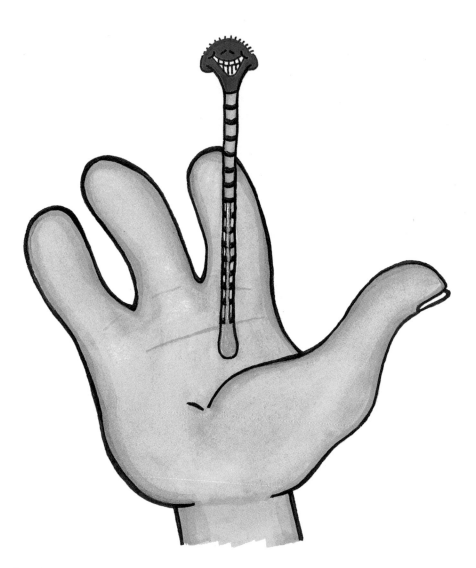

"Hey! Check me out!" hollered another tall, skinny instrument. "No one ever pays attention to **ther-mo-meters**."

"I'm sorry," said the boy. He hadn't meant to be rude. "What do **ther-mo-meters** do?"

26

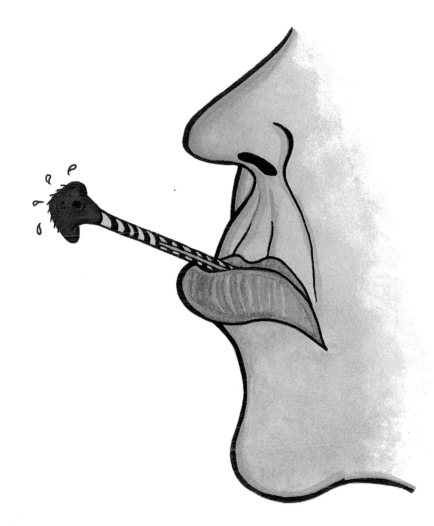

"More than happy to tell you," answered the ther-mo-meter, who was brightening up. "Hut hummm. I'm Tempo. I can tell if your body is hot, which means it's trying to fight off teeny tiny germs that make you feel bad. When you are hot, you have a fever."

"Wow," said the boy. "I thought you guys would all hurt, but so far you are definitely cool! Is that all of you?"

"If I may be so bold..." said the last instrument. He seldom spoke because he used all of his energy to keep tongues down.

28

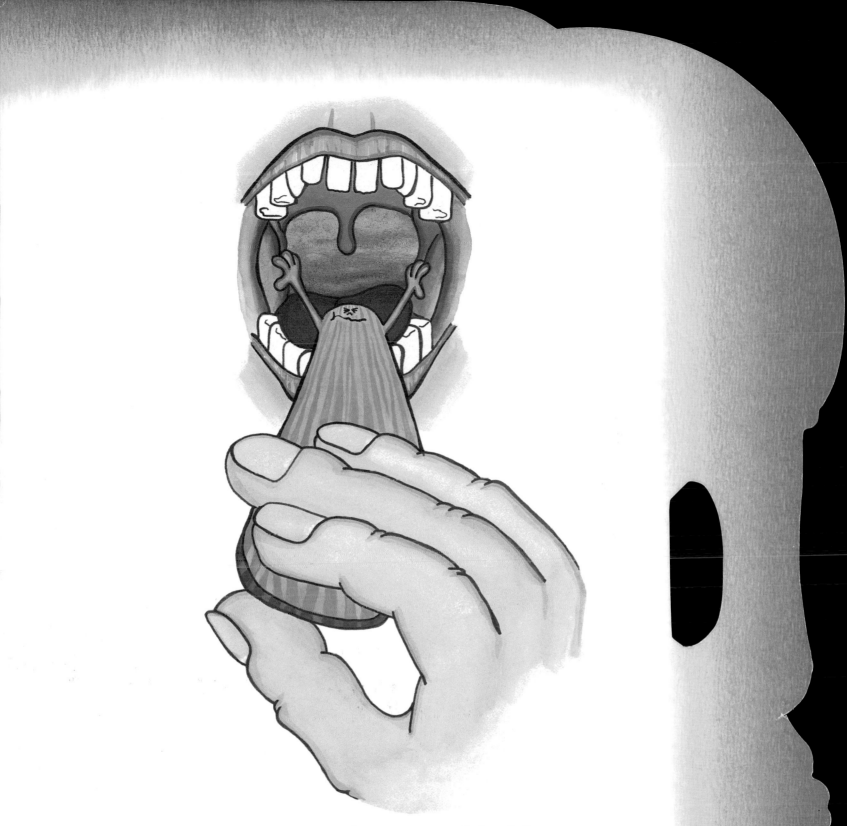

"I'm Woody, the tongue depressor. I hold your tongue down so the doctor can see way back in your throat to see why it's sore."

Just then, the head of Otis the o-to-scope plopped off again. Ms. Kneeknocker, with the help of the other instruments, lightly tapped Otis' head back on straight.

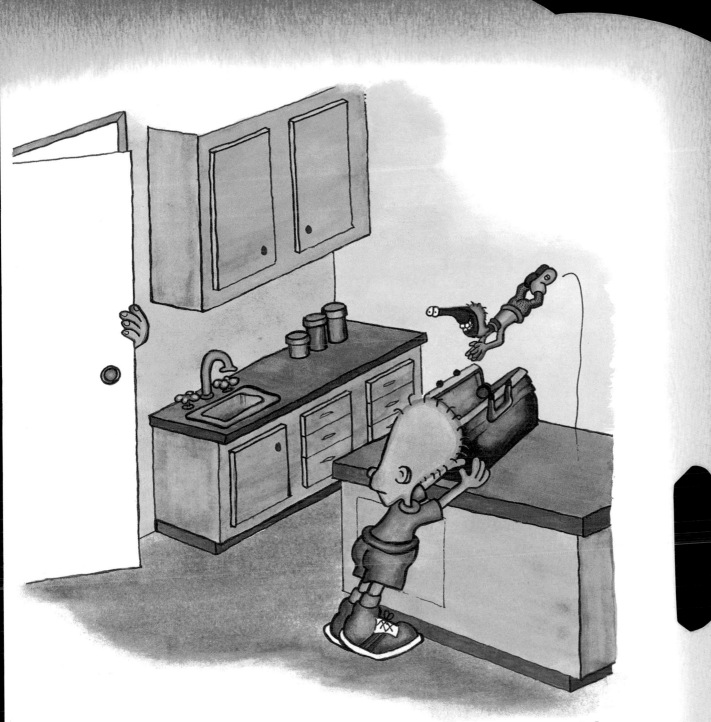

All of a sudden, everyone heard a noise outside the door.

"It's the doctor!" the instruments cried in unison. "Back into the bag! Quick!"

The boy put the doctor's black bag back on the table.

"Do you have any questions you want to ask before I examine you?" inquired the doctor of the big little boy.

"No. I'm just curious to know if my electrical system is working and if the backs of my eyes are healthy and if there are any germs in my ears, if my throat's sore or my blood pressure is ..." the boy went on.

"How did you know all *that*?!" asked the doctor, confused.

"The instruments told me," said the boy.

"Oh. I see," the doctor chuckled.

"Shall we have a look at those ears?" asked the doctor as he took his old o-to-scope out of his black bag.

"Wait a minute! Wasn't this broken?"

The boy smiled and winked at the reflex hammer who was peeking out of the black bag.

Ms. Kneeknocker winked back.

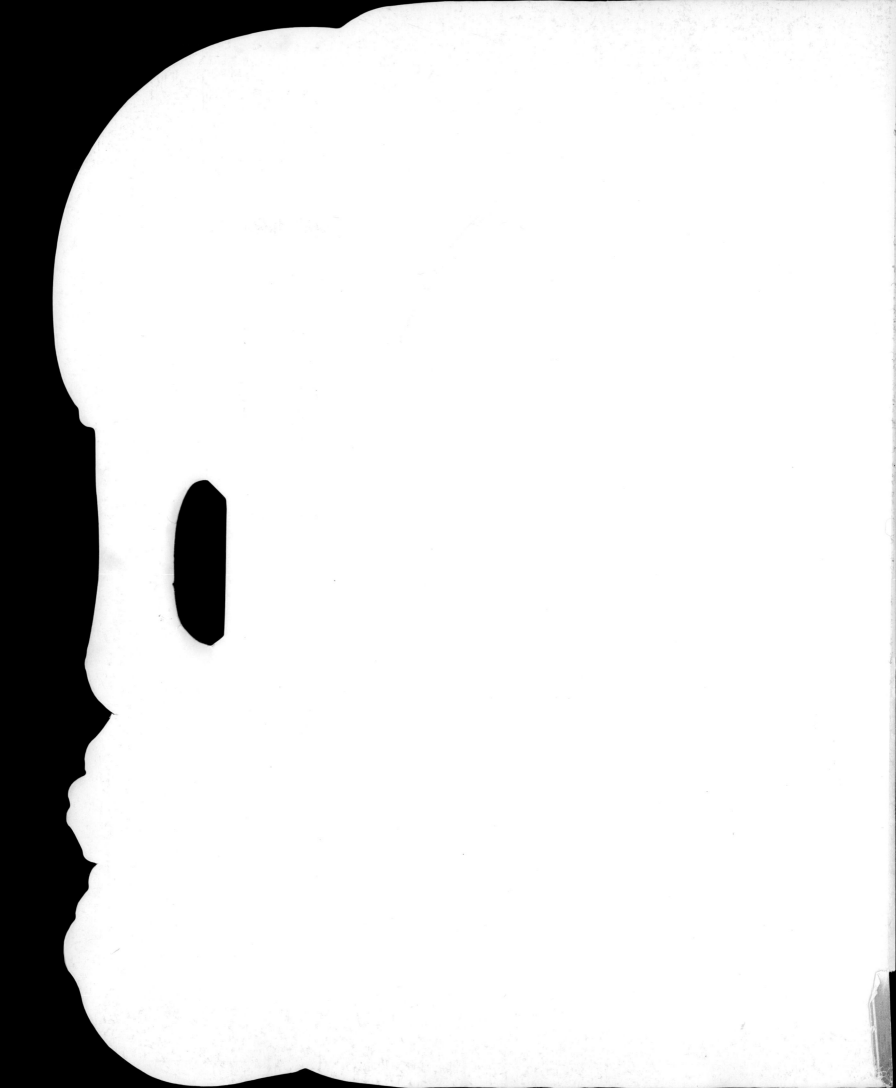